YOUR SWEATER IS UGLIER THAN MINE

SMALL-TOWN ROMANTIC COMEDY

TERRA KELLY

BALTO CREATIVE MEDIA

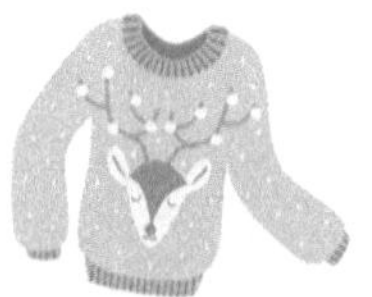

"Hot stuff coming through." I held up a sheet pan full of bagels and weaved around Anika and Molly, sitting by the wooden prep table.

"Hot stuff is right." Molly whistled and moved her legs to the side.

"Not me, the bagels." I giggled and set the pan on the table. The pan had to be propped up on one side because the indentation in the antique table was so defined.

Knead A Little Love was located in the center of town. Like the table, it was one of the oldest bread bakeries in Crystal Shores. We even used a sourdough starter that was over a hundred years old.

"Oops, my mistake." Molly laughed and jumped up to wrap her arms around my waist to give me a side hug. "You are becoming a pro with those bagels. You better be careful, Anika; Jackson could start to notice."

"Not going to happen." Anika smiled.

"Plus, that man only has eyes for her." I slid the bagels off the pan and onto a cooling rack. "Have you seen the way he looks at her?" I glanced at Molly.

"Smart man." Molly ran over to stop a timer that had just beeped. "Jasper is going to be so excited tonight." She pulled out a pie from the oven.

"Oh, what did he do to deserve your award-winning pie?" I bumped my hip against Anika. "Or what will he be doing?"

"You are officially a part of the family with *that* question." Anika burst out laughing. "Molly, care to elaborate?"

"Can't he just be amazing?"

"No," Anika and I answered at the same time.

Chaos. That was my life: chaos and fun.

Ten months ago, I closed my eyes and randomly pointed my finger on a Michigan map to find a new place to live. I was born and raised in a suburb of Detroit, but I was ready for a change. My finger landed right on Crystal Lake, next to a small town called Crystal Shores. I had never heard of the town, but after researching the area and looking through photo after photo, I wanted to know more.

I caught a sign for fresh, hot bagels when I arrived in town.

Ten months later, I was becoming a pro at making those same bagels.

"How is it possible Christmas is a month away?" Anika grabbed a mixing bowl. "Willow, did you see they're looking for people to help decorate the downtown area?"

"Oh, that would be a great way to meet more locals." Molly placed the chocolate lemon chess pie in a box and closed the lid. "I think Mack from Snuggle-In helps out every year."

"Mack?" By the sound of the name, I thought Molly was trying to set me up with a guy.

"Mackinac, she's Holland and Jenison's younger sister."

"Oh, I thought..."

"It was a guy." Molly laughed. "She's in charge of the rescue at Snuggle-In, if you're looking for a furry companion." She winked.

My first instinct was to say no. My parents were not animal people, so I didn't have an animal growing up. Since this was the year of change, maybe I needed to think about taking a trip to the shelter.

"Well, maybe."

"Why are you hesitating?" Anika grabbed the vanilla extract off the little shelf in front of me. "Are you not an animal person?"

"Honestly, I have no idea." I shrugged. "We didn't have animals growing up."

"I can't imagine not having an animal in my life." Molly rested her hands on the prep table.

"Let me think about it." I grabbed the oven mitt and made my way back to the oven. "For both the animal and decorating."

"Mack is always looking for volunteers to spend time with the cuties." Molly kissed my cheek. "See you both tomorrow." She held the pie box up and winked. "Not too early, though."

"TMI," Angie yelled and then turned toward me. "I guess I just assumed, but do you celebrate Christmas?"

"Yes, but in my family, it was always low-key." I grabbed another pan of bagels from the oven. "My mom hated to decorate. She would do the bare minimum for my brother and me."

"So, if this is the year of change..."

"I should go crazy with the decorations."

"Exactly."

I placed the hot pan on the table. "Huh, that does sound fun."

"Wait—" she grabbed my forearm— "I should throw an ugly Christmas sweater party."

"That's a thing?" I knew I sounded confused.

"Yes, and it would be such a great way for you to meet several of our friends." She clapped her hands together and picked up the spatula to continue mixing a batter. "Molly may go a little crazy with this idea."

"Because she likes parties?"

"Because she keeps talking about how you need to meet more people."

"Got it." I laughed, grabbed some cooled bagels to carry up front, and put them in the display case. The bell above the door rang, and a guy walked in. "Welcome. How can I help you?" I lifted my head for a split second and finished with the bagels.

"Hi." He was slowly walking the length of the display. "Damn, you're already sold out of the stollen bread."

"We did. Someone bought the last one about an hour ago." I straightened and leaned my forearms on the end of the cabinet. That's when I finally noticed *him*. Holy shit. His dark green eyes almost took my breath away.

"Are you going to have some tomorrow?" He shoved his hands in his pants pockets.

"We will. Every day this month. Do you want to place an order so you don't miss out again?"

"Andy," Anika said from behind me. "It's good to see you."

"Hey, Anika." He smiled, and I placed my hand over my chest to keep from making a sound. I had met a lot of guys in town, but something about *this* guy had woken up my girl parts.

"He was just asking about the stollen bread." I removed

my hand from my chest and laced my fingers together in front of me.

"Oh, yeah, that's right." She nodded. "You're offering it at the bar, right?"

"Yeah. Maybe I should place an order for every day this month."

"I'll grab an order form." I needed to leave the room. There was something about him. The order forms were in a book in the back. I stood at the shelf and took a few deep breaths before letting them out slowly.

"You okay." Anika stepped up beside me.

"What? Yeah. Totally." I reached for the book.

"I told him we'll add his information." Anika handed me a pen. "He's a bartender at Lakeside Pub." She turned her head to the side. "Willow, you're flushed. Did something happen?"

"*He* walked into the bakery."

"Oh!" She grabbed my hand. "Oh, wait, and I never introduced you to him."

She walked back up front, but I grabbed her hand. "No. Wait. Next time."

"Are you sure?"

"100%."

"Okay, next time."

When I moved here ten months ago, I wasn't interested in finding a boyfriend, but it was safe to say times had changed.

TWO

ANDY

"They're sold out," I said, as I leaned against the doorframe of Julian's office–the owner of Lakeside Pub. "Do you have a backup plan?"

"Shit." He stopped typing and shook his head. "Fuck. I can't believe I forgot to grab some on the way in this morning."

"Anika added us to the order sheet for every day this month." I shrugged. "Which, I know, doesn't help us for tonight."

"They'll have to go without." Julian started typing again. "It's only one day."

"Okay." I pushed off the doorframe and took one step before stopping. "Hey, did you know someone is helping Anika in the bakery?"

"Who? Willow?" Julian never looked up. "She's not new. I think she's been there since the beginning of the year. Why?"

"No reason." There was no point in continuing the conversation when Julian worked on the computer. He was a great guy, except when he had to deal with monthly numbers. "I'll find a replacement for the stollen bread tonight."

For the whole month of December, we served Glüh-wein, a German mulled wine, paired with a slice of stollen bread for a unique touch. The bread perfectly complemented the warm drink with its fruit, spices, and marzipan center.

I stood in the center of the dry storage room, trying to think about a replacement for the bread, when I heard a knock at the back door.

They knocked again. "I'm coming." I pushed the door open. "Yeah." It was *her*—the woman from the bakery.

"Hi, sorry to bother you."

"Willow, right?" I pushed the door open further. "Andy."

"It's nice to meet you." She smiled.

She was holding a bag with both hands. "Anika found this in the freezer for you tonight?" She handed me the bag.

"What is it?"

She paused before answering. "Fruit cake."

"American fruit cake?"

"Um, yeah." I stared at the bag before adding, "If you don't want it, we understand." She stepped forward and reached for the bag.

"It should be fine." I took a step back. "Come on in." There was a prep table in the middle of the room. "Well, I think it will be fine, but I don't know if Julian will agree."

"What am I not agreeing to?" Julian stepped out of his office and made his way over to the prep table. "It's nice to see you again, Willow."

"Same to you." She smiled. "Anika found a fruit cake in the freezer and wanted you to have it."

"American fruit cake?" Julian opened the bag, pulled

the cake out, and groaned. "I'll say it's okay if you both agree to one thing?"

"Sure." I knew exactly what he meant.

Willow glanced my way, and I nodded. "Um, okay."

"My brother can never know we served American fruit cake." He closed the bag and sighed.

"Who's your brother?" I tried not to laugh at Willow's question, but she looked confused.

Julian scowled. "You've been in Crystal Shores for over a year, right?"

"Ten months."

"And you don't know my brother, August? Owner of the restaurant next door?" Julian seemed shocked.

"To be fair, I don't know you all that well, either." Willow shrugged. Julian laughed and left the room. "I hope I didn't offend him."

"Nope." I shrugged. "He doesn't offend easily."

"Good." She turned to leave. "I hope that works for tonight. Tomorrow, you can pick up your order after 9:00 a.m."

"Thank you." I stood there staring at the door as she left. You rarely meet someone living in a small town who doesn't know one of the more popular restaurants. Something about her honesty made my body react. The feeling took me by surprise.

Razem was a casual dining restaurant that served Polish and German food with some Midwest vibes. At the pub, we served some of the menu items perfect for bar food.

I glanced in the bag and groaned. The fruit cake would be too sweet for the mulled wine, but beggars can't be choosers.

Before I carried the fruit cake up front, I needed to run to the dry storage for two bottles of bourbon and a bottle of

Glühwein. The Maker's Mark bourbon was on the bottom shelf. I bent down to grab it, and at the same moment, a memory slammed into me.

I could see my ex was holding two shot glasses in front of her, and she had the biggest smile splashed across her face. We were celebrating our twelfth anniversary with shots of bourbon and butternut squash-filled ravioli.

I shook my head free of the memory and carried everything up front.

"Have you tried the cake yet?" Julian stepped up beside me.

"No, but I feel it's going to be too sweet for the mulled wine." I set the bag down and put the bottles of alcohol away. "Do you want me to serve it still?"

He grabbed a knife and cut a slice. "Let's find out." He handed me half of the slice. His reaction was hilarious. "Nope." He set the remainder of his piece on the bar.

"It's not that bad." I finished the piece. "Sweet, but it will work."

"Are you bad-mouthing my fruit cake?" Anika sat down on a barstool and rested her hands on the bar.

Julian rolled his eyes. "It's not *your* cake I don't like."

"I know." She giggled. "Fruit cake is not for everyone."

I grabbed Julian's discarded piece. "It's delicious. Your recipe is different from any I've had before."

"Why, thank you, Andy." Anika smiled. "I wanted to pop in before I headed home and tell you I'm sorry about the stollen bread."

"It's not your fault." Julian's phone beeped. "I need to grab this, but thank you for bringing the backup." He waved and disappeared into the back.

"Hey, I also wanted to apologize to you." She placed her hand on my forearm.

"Me? Why?" I had no idea what she was talking about.

"I should've introduced you to Willow earlier." She hopped off the barstool. "Especially if you're going to buy bread from us weekly."

"We met when she dropped off the backup bread." I pointed to the fruit cake.

"Good." She blew a kiss as she was leaving. "See you tomorrow morning."

Willow was stunning. Anyone with eyes could figure that out.

And my body did react when her hand grazed over mine as she passed me the fruit cake.

Then, the memory of my ex invaded my thoughts. It had been almost a year since she left, and I still found it hard to think about another woman.

After all this time, I didn't miss my ex anymore, but I did miss being with someone. Maybe it was time to get back on the horse and try again.

THREE

"Willow." Andy from Lakeside Pub rested his hand on the counter. "Good morning."

He had this way too cheerful sound to his voice. "You're a morning person, eh?" I laughed and placed the stollen bread in a pastry box.

"Well, to be fair, I woke up an hour ago." He took a step back. "I shouldn't tell you that, should I?"

I handed him the box. "You're safe. Plus, I like my job."

"Do you have a background in bread baking or pastries?" He set the box on the counter and pulled out his wallet.

"Oh, goodness, no." I rang up his order. "Anika taught me everything I know. Um–" I pointed at the box– "two things. Do you want to pay for everything at the end of the month since you need them daily? And do you need one or two loaves?"

"That would be great if we could get a bill for everything." He put his money back in his wallet. "Right now, we only need one loaf. That may change a week or two before Christmas."

"Just let us know, and we'll adjust your order." The bell rang, and a woman walked into the bakery. "I'll be right with you."

Andy turned and smiled. "Mackinac, it's been way too long." Mack made an excited sound and hugged him.

"Andy." She glanced my way and back at Andy. "What did you buy me?" She winked and tapped on the box.

"Freshly baked stollen bread." He had the box close to his chest and moved away from her. "If you want *this*, you'll need to order some Glühwein at the pub."

"Oh, I see how you are." She smiled and leaned her hip on the display case. "Maybe I'll make that happen before the end of the month."

"Bring Jenison and Holland, too." Andy turned toward me. "Thank you, Willow." He attempted to leave when Mack grabbed his bicep.

"Wait, I popped in to see Willow, but you might be interested." Mack clapped her hands in excitement. "Molly mentioned you might want to help put up the Christmas decorations in the downtown area, Willow. Is that true?"

I thought about it yesterday when Molly and Anika mentioned it, but I haven't considered it since. "Um, they told me about how you might need help."

"It would be amazing if you—" she looked at Andy— "both could help. We're short a few hands this year."

I wasn't against the opportunity, and working alongside Andy was intriguing. "What are the hours?" My day started at the bakery early; I was like a pumpkin at 7:00 every evening.

"This Saturday and Sunday from 9:00 am to 3:00 pm." She clasped her hands together and held them against her chest. "Please say yes."

"Sure." I was off this weekend, which meant I would be sitting on the couch flipping through baking shows and cheesy romance movies. Getting out of the house sounded perfect.

"Really?" She grabbed my hand and squeezed it. "Andy, what about you?"

"I start work at 11:00 am on Saturday." Mack's face fell. "Julian might fill in for me, though."

"Seriously." She was still holding my hand and now grabbed his. "I'm so glad I caught you both at the same time." She squeezed our hands and jumped up and down once. "It's going to be so much fun." It looked like she was floating toward the door; she seemed so happy.

"Mack, I do have a question for you." I didn't think about the decorating last night, but I woke up from a dream where I had rescued two kittens. I couldn't get them out of my mind.

"Yes." She leaned against the side of the door.

"Molly and Anika mentioned you run the rescue at Snuggle-In."

"Are you about to tell me more good news?" Her face lit up.

"Um, I don't know." I laughed. "I've never had an animal, but I'm curious." She threw her hand over her mouth, and her eyes went wide. "Oh, is that bad since I've never had one?"

"Bad." She ran back to the counter and grabbed my hands. "No, it's amazing."

"Oh, so should I stop by Snuggle-In?"

"I'll be there bright and early tomorrow morning. I would love to introduce you to some of our rescues." She ran back to the front door. "Okay, this stop went way better than I anticipated. Now I need to get my booty back to the clinic." She waved. "See you tomorrow, Willow. Bye, Andy."

"Is she always that cheerful?" I was still watching Mack as she slid into the driver's seat of her car.

"Pretty much." Andy laughed and started to leave. "Now I need to know if you adopt an animal."

I burst out laughing. "Okay, but I'm just visiting the animals."

"That's what they all say." His hand was on the doorknob. "The last time I said those words, I came home with a dog." He waved and left.

"Oh, good, Andy got his order." Anika was just arriving for the day.

"He did, and Mackinac stopped in, too."

"Oh, did she have an order?" Anika scowled as if she were thinking about all the orders.

"No, Molly hinted that I might be interested in helping decorate the downtown area." I shook my head. "She roped Andy into the decorating, too."

"Oh, she's good." Anika washed her hands and started to fiddle with the pastries. She moved them closer to the front of the case so customers could see them better.

"And..." I paused for dramatic effect. "I'm going to Snuggle-In to meet some of her rescues."

"Ahhhh, are you?" She ran over and grabbed my hands. "Whoever ends up going home with you will be so lucky."

"I'm just visiting. I didn't say I was taking one home."

"You will. Trust me."

"I have no idea what I'm doing, so no, I won't." I laughed.

"Should we bet on this?" She wiggled her eyebrows up and down.

"What are you betting on?" Molly walked up front and

leaned her hip on the counter. I updated her on the conversation. "Oh, I'm all in on this one. Bring photos tomorrow, too."

"You both suck." I let out an exasperated sigh and went to the back to prep some bread. I could hear them laughing as the door to the walk-in cooler closed behind me.

The thought of adopting a living creature scared the hell out of me.

Continuing to go home to an empty house every night was worse.

FOUR

ANDY

"You're picking up the bread next time." I was joking, of course.

"Uh oh, what now?" Julian walked out of his office and leaned against the prep table.

"Mack popped in to talk to Willow about decorating the downtown area." I set the box with the stollen bread on the table. "And now I'm helping with decorating, too." Julian burst out laughing. "I'm glad you find that amusing."

"Mack stopped here last night and tried to rope me into the festivities." Julian opened the lid of the box. "I told her I was too busy with our events at the bar."

"What events?" I had no idea what he was talking about.

"You know..."

"So, you lied to her?" I was the one laughing now.

"Well, now that you say it that way." He crossed his arms over his chest.

"Does that mean you might have some time available this weekend?" I winked and grabbed the box with the loaf to carry up front to the bar.

"Hey, you." That voice was familiar. I set the stollen bread on a shelf and turned around. It was my ex's best friend, Elise. "I was wondering if you were working today."

"Elise. Hi." I rested my hand on the bar. She was drinking a cocktail already. "Do you need a refill or anything?"

"Nope, just one for me." She laughed and took a sip of the drink. "So, how are you?"

"Good." This was awkward. "You?"

"In the 'I hate men' category right now."

"Oh, and yet, you're talking to me."

She shrugged her shoulders. "You're Andy. It's different."

"Um, okay." I noticed someone at the other end of the bar waiting to order. "It was good to see you." Now, here I was, the one lying. It sounded nice, though.

"You, too." Her voice sounded slurred.

I started to walk away but stopped. "Elise, are you safe to drive home?"

"I'm walking home." She smiled. "Thank you for asking."

Julian stepped up behind me as I walked away and grabbed my elbow. "Is she driving home?"

"No, walking."

"Good." He patted my back.

I loved this town. You could love or hate someone; it didn't matter, and people stayed neutral and offered help.

The guy at the end of the bar looked like he had one too many, too. He was struggling to stay on his chair and kept mumbling something incoherent. What was happening today? "Can I get you some coffee?"

The guy scowled. "Coffee? In a bar?"

"You might be surprised by how much we serve daily." I

grabbed a rag and some sanitizer, rung it out, and wiped the counter off. "How are you doing today?" The guy looked pissed, but when I asked the question, he paused for a few beats. "Everything okay?"

"You know, you're the first person who asked me how I'm doing today." He rested his hands on the wooden surface.

"That can't be true." I threw the towel back in the bucket and rested my elbow on the bar.

"It is." He nodded. Then he just started unloading about his wife, kids, and money for the next several minutes.

This was the reason I liked my job—this random guy.

He walked in here ready to drink his sorrows away, and I came along and asked the right question.

Julian must've overheard me ask about coffee because I noticed him start a new pot.

Everyone who worked at Lakeside Pub knew the drill. Grab a mug of coffee if someone looked two sheets to the wind.

I grabbed a mug and filled it with fresh coffee. "Can you offer some to Elise down there?" I pointed to the woman trying to tap something on her phone. She kept tapping violently and then let out an exasperated sigh.

"On it." Julian nodded.

The guy bent his head and rested his hands on his forehead. I slid the mug under his nose. "What the..." Then he smiled and pulled the coffee closer. "Thank you."

"You're welcome."

I walked over to where Julian was standing. "Two people right after we opened. Are the holidays already starting to affect people?"

"Yeah, I guess you could say that." He leaned against the back counter. "I thought you should know."

"Uh oh, this sounds serious." I leaned against the counter next to him.

"I called Mack and apologized."

"Oh, does that mean you're helping us on Saturday and Sunday?"

"No, because you are."

"You could get someone else to cover." I winked. "Or did you create another lie?"

"Suck it." He pushed off the bar and walked away.

I tried not to laugh, but it was way too much fun. Especially because I had a funny feeling he had a crush on Mackinac.

"Hey." The guy at the end of the bar had his wallet in one hand and took a drink of his coffee.

"Yeah." I took a few steps over to him. "You good?"

"I am." He stood and reached out his hand for me to shake. "I live outside of Traverse City but wanted to go somewhere away from my hometown."

"Oh, welcome to Crystal Shores." I smiled.

"They say there are reasons why we choose to do things, and you're my reason today." He handed me a twenty-dollar bill. "I needed this cup of coffee." He set the mug down in between us. "I called my wife, and she's coming to pick me up."

"That's really good." I grabbed the mug and watched him leave.

"I guess that's why you didn't want to leave this tiny town, huh?" Elise leaned her arms on the back of the chair occupied by the guy.

"Why's that?" I was curious what her answer would be.

"You're a good man with a big heart. I get it." She smiled. "Look at how you just helped that guy."

"Maybe. I hope." Being a bartender was unique. It wasn't always about serving alcohol.

"She was an idiot to leave you." She waved as she left the pub. Her words took me by surprise. That was her best friend she was talking about.

I moved to Crystal Shores to get some distance from my family—not too much, but just enough. I knew it was the best decision I could make, and leaving was never an option.

FIVE

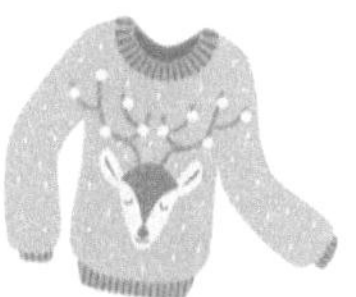

WILLOW

"What was I thinking?" I had my hand on the door to Snuggle-In Rescue. "I've never taken care of a living creature."

"Are you giving yourself a pep talk out here?" Mackinac was behind me.

"Mack." I turned around. "Hi."

"You're here bright and early." She unlocked the door and opened it. "I have a feeling your future bestie awaits just beyond those doors."

"I thought you were already here." I stepped into the lobby and immediately noticed the smell of wet hair, a cleaning agent, and the intense sounds of barking and meows echoing off every wall.

"Nope." She patted my shoulder as she passed by. "There are people here working, but in a small town, there's no reason to start at the crack of dawn."

I stood motionless in the middle of the space and glanced around. It was weird; I felt so nervous. How was it possible to feel so much unease about a tiny living creature?

The thought sparked a memory.

"Whose cat is that?" My mom pointed to the black cat sitting on the sidewalk.

"I don't know." The cat always stopped by to say hi when I came home from school. It never attempted to go on our porch or in our house. "It's so sweet." I ran my hand over the soft fur.

"Until it bites you," she harped.

"It's never bitten me before." I shrugged and continued to pet it.

"You have homework. Get inside." She groaned and walked back into the house.

I patted its head and hopped up. "See you tomorrow." I waved at the cat as I hopped up the steps.

The black cat eventually stopped coming around. I don't know if something happened to it, but I remember feeling sad when it didn't greet me every afternoon.

"Willow." Mack's voice brought me back to the present.

"Huh." I shook my head free of the thoughts. "Yeah."

"You ready?" She rubbed her hands together in anticipation and hopped up and down twice.

"Why do you look like you just received an award that consists of cake?" I pointed at her hands.

She pulled me closer. "Willow."

"Yes."

"Do you know how much I love animals?"

"I think I can ballpark it."

"Okay, good." She squeezed my hands. "So, when I know someone has never had an animal but wants to explore options..."

"You are like a kid in a candy store right after they refilled the supplies." I nodded in understanding.

"Exactly." She jumped up and down again and turned to walk down the hallway while still holding my hand. "I think I know what's going to happen today, but I don't want to jinx it."

"How could you possibly know?" I laughed. "Never mind, pretend I didn't say that."

She stopped at a door that read kittens. "Okay. Are you ready?"

"I think so." I took a deep breath and let it out as we walked into the room. The sound was almost deafening. The kittens were crying their disdain for being locked up. Several of them stretched out their paws and tried to grab onto whatever was within reaching distance. My shoulder was a perfect object for one of the kittens. The contact made me pause, and something happened; my mood shifted.

"Uh oh, they're already fighting over you." Mack grabbed the kitten's paw and kissed it. "Hey, cutie."

I stood before the kitten's cage, which demanded my attention, and stared at the dark gray and white baby for several long seconds.

"What's this one's name." I played with its paws as the kitten continued to reach toward me.

Mack pointed to the paper right below the cage door. "Frank." She laughed. "This little man was found all alone behind the hardware store."

"How is that possible? Could there be siblings somewhere?" I beeped his nose, and he attempted to bite the tip of my finger.

"We suspect because Crystal Shores is a small town, people will dump the animal and keep driving." Mack took a few steps to the right. "I found these three in a dumpster behind a clothing store." She opened the cage to lean in and play with the calico kitten. "I'm still trying to decide if this one is going home with me."

"How many animals do you have at home?" I had this vision of animals running wild all over her house.

"Just one dog." She shrugged. "I lost a few in the last couple of years."

"Well, in that case, you have to adopt it." I scratched behind the kitten's ears. "What happens if you separate them? Won't they miss each other?"

"The calico is a loner. It's always doing its own thing. "These two–" she tickled their tummies– "are besties."

I slowly turned around in a full circle to get a full picture of who was in the room. At the opposite end from where I stood, in a bottom cage, a kitten was cleaning its paws. This particular kitten caught my attention because it sat next to a puppy playing with a chew toy.

I walked over and squatted down in front of the cage. "There's a puppy in the kitten room."

"Crazy, right?" She laughed and bent down beside me. "They were owner released and bonded to each other."

"How long have they both been here?" The kitten stopped cleaning and stared at me. I placed my hand on the cage, and it lunged forward and tried to attack my hand. The puppy lifted its head in curiosity.

"Um, about a week." Mack sat on the floor and crossed her legs in front of her. "They are so chill but still so much fun." The cat was all black and reminded me of the cat who visited me as a child. "Do you want to hold them?"

"Yeah, I do." I sat down beside Mack.

She pulled the kitten out first. "Hold on." The kitten squirmed in her hands. "Someone wants to meet you." She turned and placed her in my lap. Then, she grabbed the puppy and sat down beside me. "You look like you've seen a ghost."

I ran my finger down the bridge of the kitten's nose and

sighed. "You could say that," I told her about the cat from my childhood. "It's silly, I know."

"Nope, not at all." She kissed the top of the puppy's head. "That's why I encourage people to give themselves time when finding a new animal." The puppy jumped out of her lap and onto mine. "Sometimes a bond is made long before you even meet." She laughed. "I think this is one of those moments."

The kitten licked the dog's head, and they both snuggled together on my lap. "I've never taken care of a living creature in my life. Not even a fish."

"You did bond with that black cat, though." She smiled.

"That's true."

"And you moved here because it was time to make a few changes in your life, right?"

"Yeah." Mack knew about my strained relationship with my mom.

"What if they're a part of that change?" She pointed at the two animals, now sound asleep on my lap.

"That thought should freak me out."

"But it doesn't?"

I shook my head no and placed my hands on their backs. Me, caring for not one but two living creatures.

Moving to Crystal Shores was about letting go of my past and creating new beginnings.

SIX

WILLOW

"What the?" Two sets of eyes were staring at me, and their little bodies were sitting perfectly in the middle of my chest. "Well, good morning to you." I reached up and ran my hands down their backs.

Less than twelve hours ago, I adopted not one but two animals. I had walked into the rescue with plans to maybe adopt an animal. I wanted to talk to Mackinac first about the possibilities.

Leaving with a kitten and puppy was not part of the plans.

"Aren't you supposed to be in the playpen we set up last night?" I playfully pulled at their ears and tickled their sides.

They were given names at the rescue, but it did not work for me to call them Monica and Rachel. When they were playing last night, I thought about Broccoli and Cauliflower or Buddy & Holly. But they didn't feel right, so we put name ideas on hold until today.

"Have you thought about the names we discussed?"

Puppy hopped off the bed, but I had to pick up the kitten and move her down by my feet to pull the covers back. "Hey." They both stopped hopping around and stared at me. "What if we thought of Christmas names? You are my Christmas babies."

My phone buzzed with a text message.

Mack: Did you survive the night?
Me: Somehow, yes.
Mack: Are you accepting visitors this early? (Winking emoji)

A second later, I heard a knock on the door.

"Let's see if Auntie Mack can help us pick a name for you two." They followed behind me as I made my way toward the door. "Good morning." When the door opened, Kitten and Puppy tried to escape, but Mack reached down and scooped them up.

"Well, hello there." She kissed their noses. "Seriously, you scored with these two."

I reached for the kitten. "Except when they are plotting their escape. Want some coffee?"

"More than life itself." She set the puppy down and followed me into the kitchen. "How was your first night?"

"I woke up with two fluff balls on my chest." I grabbed the coffee grounds from the cabinet

"Didn't you plan to keep them in a playpen?" She sat down on a barstool.

"I did. They had other plans." I poured water into the pot. Mack laughed. "It's funny, yesterday, I was freaking out about caring for a living thing. Today, I'm more stressed about finding that perfect name."

"Oh, I love that." She rubbed her hands together. "Tell me some of your ideas?"

We spent an hour drinking coffee and trying to find the perfect names for them.

The contenders were sugar and spice, cinnamon and nutmeg, and cookie and holly.

"Cookie and Holly are damn cute names." I sat on the floor and patted the carpet, trying to get their attention. The kitten was currently licking the puppy's head. "Hey, you." The puppy jumped up and ran toward me. "I think you should be Cookie because of your dark brown spots."

Mack joined me on the floor. "You do look like a chocolate chip cookie." She ran her hand up and down the puppy's back. "I'm so curious about its breed. It's a mystery." The puppy had medium hair and was tan with dark brown spots in several areas.

"My luck, it will be a large breed." I laughed and playfully made the puppy fall onto its back. "My first time having a dog, and I'll end up with a Great Dane mix."

"She will be your protector." Mack reached for the kitten. "So, that means you are Holly." The kitten batted at her hands. "Do you like the name Holly?" The kitten lunged forward and did this roll and twist before grabbing her hand. "Wow, I'm going to take that as a yes."

"Cookie and Holly," I said the names out loud. "Just like you two—" I grabbed them both and brought them close to my chest— "those names make me happy."

"Another rescue success." Mack hopped up from the floor. "Make sure to take a few photos so I can add them to the website."

After she left, I thought about getting in the shower and

maybe starting laundry. Instead, I didn't move from the floor for a few hours. At one point, I fell asleep and woke up to Cookie and Holly snuggled against my chest.

There were days when I thought about moving back home. Even though I wasn't close to my family and my mom wasn't interested in talking to me, I still felt this need to be close to them.

I knew that's what made me different from them.

Crystal Shores continued to surprise me. The town felt like one big warm hug, and the people made me feel special.

Cookie stretched her legs out and yawned. Then she hopped up and started to lick my face. "Do you think you both need a treat?" Holly's eyes flew open, and she sat up. "I guess that's a yes, eh?"

They followed me to the kitchen. "Let's see what we have in here." I rummaged around in a bag as they circled my feet. "Oh, look." I had a treat in each hand. "I have a funny feeling you're both going to be very spoiled."

My fear about caring for a living creature had been replaced with excitement.

Cookie grabbed the treat, ran into the living room, and hopped on the couch. "How the heck did you jump up there so easily? I'm impressed." Holly ate her treat right next to my feet. I reached down and scratched behind her ears.

At that moment, I realized I was done worrying about the family who stopped caring about me years ago. It was time to focus on the new little family I was creating here in Crystal Shores.

SEVEN

ANDY

"You look exhausted." I tried not to laugh as Willow yawned. "Good thing I brought you this." I held up a cup of coffee.

"Bless you." Willow grabbed the cup with both hands and pulled it toward her chest. "I had no idea a puppy and kitty could have so much energy." She yawned again. "They can go for hours before they finally crash."

"So, I guess that means you did adopt an animal. Well, two animals." I smiled and took a sip of my coffee.

"It was hard to say no." She shrugged her shoulders and pulled out her phone. "Would you be able to say no to those faces?"

"Oh, um, no." I grabbed her phone to get a closer look. "What made you adopt a puppy and a kitten?"

"They were together in a cage."

"Seriously?"

"Yeah, someone brought them in together." She put her nose over the opening to the to-go cup lid and breathed in the aromas. "They're bonded. I loved that the rescue didn't separate them. You should see them at home; they go everywhere together."

"I would love to meet them." I was so impressed at how Willow was nervous to have an animal but gave not one but two animals a home. "Maybe they can have a play date with my dog."

"How big is your dog?" She turned her head to the side, obviously curious about my answer.

"Queensland Heeler mix. He's about 45 pounds."

"Oh, that's not bad, but we should wait a few more months." She laughed. "They're still pretty tiny." She placed her hand on my forearm. "But you can still meet them."

"I look forward to it." I could hear Mackinac's voice behind us. "Sounds like it's time to decorate." I winked and turned around.

"Good morning, you two." Mack placed her hands on both of our shoulders. "Are you ready to spread some holiday spirit throughout the town?"

"Um–" I glanced over at Willow– "yes."

"What Andy said." Willow nodded.

"It's so much fun." Mack hopped up and down. "Come on." She walked over to a shed behind a building. "Everything is in here." She unlocked the doors and stepped inside. "I have a very important question. She turned to face us while holding a garland in one hand and a strand of lights in the other. Which one?"

My first instinct was to say garland, but I waited to answer. "Willow, thoughts?"

"I've been known to throw out a strand of lights if they are too tangled." She raised her eyebrows and laughed.

"So, garland it is." Mack handed the long strand to me. "Make sure she doesn't throw out any garland."

"Noted." I wrapped my hand around the large strand.

"Are there specific places where you want the garlands to be placed?" Willow stepped into the shed and grabbed some more garlands.

"We want them on lights, building signs, anywhere with a flat surface." She clapped her hands together and walked away.

"Mackinac has spoken." I laughed and headed over to a light post. "Wait, is there a ladder in the shed?"

"Yes," Willow yelled from the small space. "Grabbing it."

When we arrived, it was freezing, but it was typical Michigan weather in December. By the time we hung the last garland at 2:45 p.m., our hands and faces were like icicles.

"Please tell me we're done." I stepped down off the ladder. "I don't know if I'll have the ability to hold a garland or hammer any more nails." My gloves usually kept my hands warm, but they let me down today. Plus, the little bit of snow in places didn't help because it made my gloves wet.

"Same." She rubbed her hands together.

"Should we go get some hot chocolate at Razem?" I glanced around, hoping to find Mack somewhere nearby. "Let me text Mack to let her know we're finished and heading out."

"She was running across the street the last time I saw her." She pointed in the direction of Lakeside Pub. "Maybe we'll see her over at Razem."

We made sure to put the ladder away and lock up the shed.

"Okay, let's get out of the cold." I placed my hand in the middle of her back and walked toward the restaurant."

"I'm excited to finally try Razem."

"Oh, you're in for a treat." We waited for the cars to clear and crossed the street. "August likes to go all out when he makes anything."

"So, his hot chocolate must be amazing."

"Out of this world." I grabbed the handle and pulled the door open. "He also makes different flavored whipped cream."

"How have I not been here before?"

"That is a mystery we need to solve."

The host walked back to his station and grabbed two menus. "Hey, Andy. Just the two of you today?"

"Just us." I nodded.

He seated us in the back near the doors to the kitchen. You could hear someone yelling. "Wow, I hope everything is okay." Willow's eyes went wide as she slid into her seat.

"That's just August being August." The host laughed and placed the menus in front of us. "Your server will be here in a moment."

"August sounds angry." Willow leaned forward and whispered in case the man in question pushed open the kitchen doors.

"He does seem intense, but he's just a big teddy bear." I shrugged. It was true, too. His bark was worse than his bite.

"Andy." The loud voice from the kitchen was now behind me. "What are you doing here? Shouldn't you be next door?" He laughed and slapped his hand against my shoulder.

"Julian is filling in so I could help decorate the downtown area."

"Who roped you into that?" His eyes moved over to Willow.

"Not me." She placed her hand against her chest. "You can blame Mackinac for that."

"Sounds about right." He laughed. "Should I make a couple of hot chocolates for the occasion?"

"Yes. That's why we're here."

August pointed at Willow. "Chocolate, cherry, or peppermint?"

"Cherry."

"Great choice." He smiled and glanced over at me. "Your usual?"

"Yup."

"Your usual." Willow watched August disappear through the doors into the kitchen.

"Peppermint." I still had my gloves on because my hands were freezing. "It's the whipped cream flavor for the hot chocolate."

"Oh, cherry will pair perfectly."

"It does. I can confirm that." I rubbed my hands together to try to get them warm. "What brought you to Crystal Shores?"

"My finger." She laughed. "I closed my eyes and pointed to a place on the map."

"Crystal Shores was the winner."

"Exactly."

There was something different about Willow; she was easy to talk to. When I woke up this morning, I looked forward to the day and decorating the town with her.

Something I hadn't felt in a while.

EIGHT

WILLOW

"Holy wow, this–" I pointed at my mug– "is amazing."

"The best." Andy nodded and took another sip of his hot chocolate. When he lifted his head, he had a whipped cream mustache.

"Um." I pointed at him and, at the same time, my lip.

"I did it again." He grabbed a napkin and wiped his lip. "I think August puts an enormous amount of whipped cream on top for a reason."

"Lies." August walked over to our table.

"Are you sure about that?" Andy looked stern, but it was obvious he was struggling not to laugh.

"I'll never tell." August shrugged his shoulders. He glanced my way. "How is yours? Sorry, I forgot to ask your name."

"Willow. And it's delicious." I grabbed my spoon and pushed it down into the whipped cream.

"Isn't that cheating?" Andy had another mustache on his upper lip.

"It's better than getting a mustache." I pointed at his lip again.

"Dammit." He quickly wiped it off and grabbed his spoon. "Fine. I like your idea better."

"I don't think I've seen you here before, Willow?" August crossed his arms over his chest.

"Yeah, somehow, this is my first time." I grabbed another spoonful of whipped cream. "I have a weird schedule at Knead A Little Love."

"Anika makes the best bread." He paused for a beat. "I guess I should say you both make the best bread."

"Thank you." I had eaten enough whipped cream and could finally lift the mug and drink it like a normal person. Steam was still billowing out, so I knew it would be hot. The tiny sip I managed to enjoy hit all my senses. "Whoa." I took another sip. "This is out of this world."

"Oh, I'm glad you like it." He dropped his arms to his side.

"The cherry in the whipped cream, mixed with the dark chocolate, amazing." Holding the mug with both hands, I took little sips to savor the drink.

"That's all I need to hear. Now I can get back to work." He waved as he pushed the door to the kitchen open with his hand. "Willow, you should come in for dinner sometime. I'll make you both a special entree." Then he was gone.

"Um, can we talk about this hot chocolate?" I set the mug down and leaned back in my chair.

"It's so good. I know." He laughed and took another sip. "So, we should take him up on the offer."

"For dinner?"

"Yeah. Would you like to join me next week?"

I traced a finger around the handle of the mug. This week was full of surprises. First, Mack was so excited to have Andy and me decorate the downtown area. Then, I adopted a kitten and a puppy. Something I never thought I would do. That's not all. I was having hot chocolate with Andy, and he asked me out.

"Yes." I wrapped my hands around the mug and took a sip. "I would love that, and before we leave today, we may need to order one more hot chocolate to-go."

"I like the way you think." He nodded. "You should try the peppermint-flavored whipped cream."

"Not today. I need more of this cherry." I heard someone tsking behind me. Then Mack appeared. "You found us."

"You bailed on me." She had the saddest look on her face.

"Sit." I pointed at an empty chair. "Have you had the hot chocolate here?"

"You didn't? Which flavor of whipped cream did you order?" She grabbed my mug and took a sip. "My absolute favorite. Love cherry." She sighed. "Why did you bail?"

"We couldn't feel our hands." Andy still had his gloves on.

"Plus, we put up all the garlands." I snatched the mug back. "Well, there wasn't any more garland in the shed."

"Wow, you two are fast." She tapped her fingers on the table. "The person taking care of the lights has been fighting with the strands all afternoon. He still has half the down-town area."

"We're coming back tomorrow, right?" I thought that was the plan.

"Would you be up to finish the lights?" Her eyes lit up.

"Of course," Andy answered before me.

"You two are the best." She hopped up and kissed both our cheeks. "I need to pop in the back and beg August to make me a hot chocolate." She winked as she pushed open the door.

"That was okay to say yes, right?" He sounded cautious or maybe unsure.

"Yeah. I'll probably curse a lot when working with the lights, but yes, it's okay." I took the last sip of my hot chocolate.

"We'll be cursing together." He pushed his chair back. "I need to head over and start my shift at the pub."

"I should probably get home and see what my two furry babies have destroyed." I pushed my chair back and stood. "Do you think we can get a hot chocolate to go?"

"Let's go see." We walked to the back together.

We were a few yards from the office when we both stopped. Mack and August had their arms wrapped around each and they were kissing.

"Um, is this new, or are they dating?" I had no clue.

"New." He wrapped his hand around my bicep and walked in the opposite direction. "I thought Julian liked Mack."

"Uh oh." I covered my mouth and quickly walked back up front. "Well, that was fun."

"Our little secret." He shook his head.

"I won't say a word." I pretended to zip my lips. "Okay, since we're not getting more hot chocolate, I'm going to head home and find out what's been destroyed."

He held the front door open for me. "I'll see you tomorrow at 9:00 am?"

"With bells on." I laughed and turned to leave.

"Willow."

"Yeah." I glanced over my shoulder.

"I had a lot of fun today." He waved and turned to leave.

"Me, too." My car was a block away, and the temperature had dropped several degrees. I found myself wishing I could snuggle against Andy to warm up.

That was a new thought, and I wasn't opposed to the idea.

NINE

ANDY

"What are you doing?" My dog, Sammy, was sitting right in front of the TV. It looked like he was watching the show. "Are you a fan, too?" Sammy hopped up and ran over to me. "Should we go for a quick walk before I leave?"

Usually, when I said "walk," his ears would perk up, and he would jump up and down. Not today, though. Instead, my dog actually ran down the hall and into my bedroom.

"What is this craziness?" I followed him into the bedroom. "You always go for a walk." Sammy was snuggled on the bed with his head down. "Wow, is it too cold for a walk?" He did run out and pee in record time for the morning potty break.

I kissed the top of his head and finished getting ready.

A small part of me would've loved to join Sammy and not decorate downtown today, but a bigger part of me was excited to spend the day with Willow.

Several women had tried to get my attention at the pub,

but I had worked hard to avoid all female contact. I wasn't ready. After spending twelve years with one woman, the thought of dating someone else made me want to hide deep under the covers, just like Sammy.

Until I met Willow.

She was different.

We talked, laughed, and enjoyed each other's company. No expectations were needed.

It took me ten minutes to drive into town. It snowed last night and was much colder today. If my hands were numb yesterday, I could only imagine how bad they would be today.

I noticed Willow getting out of her car as I pulled into a parking spot. "Good morning." I quickly rolled my window down to get her attention.

"Andy." She flashed the biggest smile. "Good morning." She held up a bag. "I have a surprise for you."

"A surprise for me?" I hit the lock button for my vehicle.

"It was a spur-of-the-moment purchase." She handed me the bag. "You'll understand when you see it."

"Okay." I opened the bag and laughed. "I was just thinking about how cold my hands would be today." I held up the gloves.

"Not anymore." She wiggled her fingers. "They're the best. Try them on."

I slid one on. "Wait, is that fur inside?"

"Yes." She clapped her hands together. "And the outside is waterproof."

"Where did you find them?" I rubbed my hands together.

"I looked online, but the delivery time was two days. I knew we needed them today, so I popped into the hardware store to see if they had any." She smiled. "They had just received the shipment a couple of days ago and already need to order more."

"Wow, now you definitely have to join me for dinner next week." I winked. "It will be my way of saying thank you."

"Will there be hot chocolate at the end of dinner?"

"Of course."

"Then, yes, it's a date." She paused. "I mean, yes, I can't wait to join you."

"For our date." I smiled and glanced behind Willow. "Mackinac is running toward us."

"Oh." She turned around. Under her breath, she whispered, "I wonder if she saw us last night?"

"My guess is no." I stepped closer to Willow and kept my voice low. "She popped into the bar half an hour after we saw her and acted like nothing happened."

"Oh." Willow's eyes widened, but she cleared her throat and tried to act normal for Mack.

"Good morning, you two." Mack typed something on her phone and then dropped her arm. "Just like I thought, we have about half the lights up. You still okay with fighting with every strand?"

"Are they that tangled?" Willow laughed.

"Pretty much." Mack rolled her eyes. "I didn't help with taking the decorations down last year. Whoever did it quickly wound them up and threw them in a box."

"I'm okay with putting up lights." I held up my gloved hands. "I won't be fighting the cold today."

"Oh, did you find those awesome new gloves at the hardware store, too?" Mack held up her hands. "I grabbed a pair right before they closed yesterday." We talked about the gloves for about five minutes. "Okay, time to focus.

Lights." She slowly walked backward and pointed in the direction of the shed. "Shed's open, lights are in a box. Keep your voice down when the cursing happens, and yes, it will happen." She waved and ran off in the opposite direction.

We made our way over to the shed. I grabbed a couple of strands of lights and turned around to face Willow. I didn't realize she was so close. We were now face to face and only a breath apart. "Um."

"Hi." She smiled.

Something happened. My body reacted. Emotions I had not felt in a while.

"Hi." My first instinct was to ignore the feelings. Then, I lifted my hand and tucked a strand of hair behind her ear; so much for ignoring shit.

We stood locked in place. Silent.

"Are they..." Mack was in the doorway.

"Here." Willow stepped back and reached down to grab a strand. "Yup."

"And they are tangled." I laughed and grabbed the other half of the strand that was tangled around several lights. "Whoever put the lights away last year should be banned from receiving Christmas gifts this year."

"I will let Eddie and Jackson know." She winked and sprinted off in the opposite direction.

"The firefighters?" Willow sounded shocked. "If anyone deserves presents, it's them."

"She was joking." I started the painstaking task of untangling every single strand. Taking care of them now made more sense and would make putting them up flow quicker. "I think."

"I hope." Willow tugged at a strand lying in the box under several layers. "We might be here for a while.

"There has to be an easier way." On impulse, I dumped everything out of the box.

"Oh, that makes sense." She bent down and pulled a little too hard at a strand of lights. Her body jerked forward, and I reached out my hands to catch her before her face met the pavement. "Shit." She wrapped her hands around my biceps.

Again, we were in an awkward position, and again, my body reacted. Without thinking, I wrapped my fingers around her neck and pulled her closer.

"Willow," I whispered and kissed her.

I thought I would regret my decision, but I didn't.

"Andy." She dropped to her knees and placed her hands flat on my chest.

"I hope that was okay?" I brushed my fingers down the side of her face.

"I hope that wasn't it." She smiled and slid her hands up my chest to wrap them around my neck.

"Of course not." I chuckled and leaned in to kiss her again. This time, we took the kiss deeper. Right as our tongues touched, someone whistled.

"I thought Mack said you were putting up lights?" Eddie was standing in the doorway of the shed. Willow jerked, and her body fell back into its sitting position on the pavement. I tried to stop her fall and fell forward onto her. "Whoa, easy now." Eddie bent down to help me up.

"Hey." I reached out to help Willow to get up. "I thought you were banned from decorating the town?"

"Banned? Really?" Eddie tucked his hands into his pants pockets. "Mack said, and I quote, if I don't help untangle the lights, I *will be* banned."

"She gave you one more shot." Willow grabbed the lights and attempted to untangle them. "I think Andy and I have it under control. It may get a little crazy with another set of hands."

"Are you sure?"

"Definitely." Willow nodded.

I nodded in agreement. I didn't say anything because my head was still spinning from our kiss. Suddenly, putting lights up in the cold didn't sound so bad.

TEN

WILLOW

"Okay, that was ridiculous." I sighed heavily and plopped down on the wooden bench a couple of feet from the shed. "We need to make sure we're the ones putting the lights away and correctly."

"We?" Andy laughed and stepped closer to the bench.

I grabbed his hand and tugged him down next to me. "Yes, we." I bumped my shoulder against his. "I'm not doing *that* without you."

"Oh." He turned his head to the side. "Mack will be happy to have volunteers already."

"Hey, you two." Mack pulled her phone against her chest. "It looks so good." She turned in a full circle, taking it all in. "How much do you hate me?"

"If we disliked anyone, it should be Eddie, not you." I smiled and hopped up. "Put our names on the list; we'll take the lights down when it's time."

"Seriously?" She jumped up and down, wrapped her arms around my waist, and pulled me in for a big hug. "Do you know how hard it is to get people to volunteer?" She stepped back and turned toward Andy. "You're okay with helping, right?"

He didn't say anything at first. His eyes were locked onto mine. A second later, he smiled. "Yeah. I am."

"Didn't Eddie help you?" She glanced around.

"He did offer, but we had it under control." I took a step closer to Andy. I silently sent Mack a message telling her why Eddie was not around. When I touched his hand, she received the message loud and clear.

"Oh, okay." She winked. "Wait, they're putting a sign up wrong." Her eyes were locked onto two figures standing by a light pole. "Thank you." She waved and ran off to fix a decoration.

"Want to get some hot chocolate?" The cherry whipped cream with hot cocoa was calling my name.

"I need to check on Sammy." He squeezed my hand.

"Sammy, your dog, right?" I turned to face him.

"Yeah, he didn't want to go for a walk this morning, and I just want to make sure he's okay."

"I wonder if he needs a play date?" I brushed my thumb back and forth over his skin.

"Oh, I forgot to ask you, how are your two new additions doing?"

"They stayed in the playpen last night."

"That's a win." Andy laughed.

I glanced down at our hands and took a step back. "You'll have to let me know when we're going out?"

"How about Thursday?"

"Sure." I didn't want our day to end, and that feeling scared me. No, not scared, but it did make me feel uncomfortable. I was still getting to know him.

A part of me wondered if I should invite him over for

the evening, which then made me wonder if he would want to spend more time with me.

The kiss was unexpected and so perfect. I could still feel his lips on mine.

I wanted him to break the awkward between us and kiss me again. He didn't, though.

"I can pick you up?" He turned to leave.

"I'll meet you at the bar." I started to take a step forward but stopped.

"Are you sure?" He seemed distracted and didn't make eye contact with me.

"Yeah." I grabbed my keys from my coat pocket. "See you soon, Andy."

His back was already turned when he waved and left.

"That was weird," I whispered to no one and walked toward my car. Instead of getting in my vehicle and driving off, I turned and went to Little Lemon Bakery. It didn't close for another two hours.

"There she is." Molly walked around the counter and pulled me in for a hug.

"Putting up Christmas lights is exhausting." I kissed her cheek and pulled out a chair to sit down.

"Like, I need a lemon bar exhausting." Molly ran back to the display.

"More like, I need a slice of chocolate lemon chess pie exhausting." I rested my forearms on the little cafe table. "Oh, and men are weird."

"Say it louder for the ladies in the back." Molly carried a small plate over and set it in front of me. "What happened?"

I shared about the kiss, our day, and the awkward goodbye.

"Do you know about his ex?" Molly sat down beside me.

"No. Is it bad?" I took a bite and moaned. "Just what the doctor ordered."

"Thank you, sweetie." Molly reached over and squeezed my hand. "He was with someone for about twelve years. I think it's been several months since she left, but still, twelve years."

"Shit. Okay, now that makes sense." I thought about the kiss. In the moment, it felt normal. Then, he had the day to think about what happened. I wondered if he regretted it.

"Hey, I bet he just needs some time to think." She leaned forward and rested her hand on the table. "That doesn't mean anything, so don't start creating scenarios in your mind."

I pushed my fork down into the last bite. "He did confirm our date on Thursday, so that's something."

"What?" She hopped up and grabbed my plate. "You forgot to tell me you had a date."

"When I told August it was my first time in Razem, he offered to make me his house special." Talking about Razem made me think about the hot chocolate. "Have you had the hot chocolate there?"

"All three flavors."

"That cherry whipped cream was out of this world." I hopped up and put on my coat. "What you're saying is, I need to try the other two flavors?"

"Um, yeah." She grabbed my hand. "Hey, don't over-think what happened today. Andy probably needs a moment to process the kiss. That's not a bad thing. His ex messed with his head."

"Thanks, Moll." I kissed her cheek and bundled up for the walk to my car.

"Willow." I was just about to my vehicle when I heard *his* voice.

"Andy." I turned around to find him standing in the middle of the sidewalk. "I thought you left."

"I did." He took a few steps forward.

"Everything okay?" I shoved my hands in my coat pockets.

"Does that offer still stand?"

"Which one? The playdate?"

"Yeah." He shrugged. "I know you wanted to wait until Holly and Cookie were bigger, but Sammy is gentle with other animals."

Well, that was interesting. I'm glad I had a chance to talk to Molly. I was willing to be more patient now that I knew more about Andy.

The kiss today surprised us both.

Him because of his past.

Me: I loved the way he made me feel. It was a warm welcome, and I wanted more.

"Yes, of course, it will be so much fun."

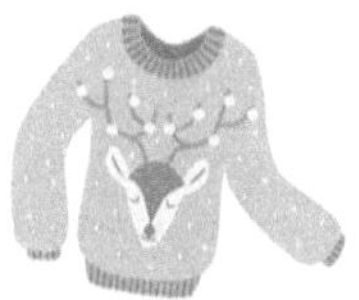

ELEVEN

"Are you kidding me right now?" I squatted down to pet Cookie and Holly. "They're so tiny."

"Right?" Willow sat down on the floor and crossed her legs in front of her. "Holly is eight weeks old, and Cookie is ten."

"What breed is Cookie? Or do they know?" I picked her up and held her against my chest. She started to lick every inch of my face. "Oh, hello. Yes, I see you."

"They have no clue, but the paperwork said Jack Russell mix." She swooped down, grabbed Holly, and held her high in the air with both hands. "It would be fun if they stayed about the same size." Holly wiggled, trying to free herself. "I have a feeling I'll end up with a medium to large breed, though."

"And the funny part is Holly would still be in control."

"So true." She laughed. We left Sammy in my car for a few minutes. I wanted to meet Holly and Cookie first. "Do you think Sammy would be okay with them?"

"Normally, he is great around other animals. If you're comfortable, we can see how he reacts." I set Cookie on the floor and hopped up. "We'll know quickly because Sammy always tells you when he's unhappy."

"Let's try." She stayed on the floor next to Cookie and Holly.

I ran outside to grab him. He was great off a leash, but I kept it on for the introduction. "Here we are." Sammy stepped through the doorway, and the two tiny animals stopped. "What do you think, Buddy?" Sammy stood rooted to the spot by the door. "Do you want to meet them?"

Holly was the brave one of the bunch and sauntered over to find out who the new creature was in her house.

"Cats. They crack me up." Willow ran her hand down Cookie's back. "Do you want to go meet Sammy?"

Holly rubbed her body against Sammy's legs. I knew my dog wouldn't hurt anyone, but my heart almost jumped through my chest when Sammy lunged forward and let out a half-bark. Then he dropped his front legs down and nudged at Holly. "Holy shit, they're playing."

Cookie ran over to join in the excitement.

Still, Sammy continued to hop around and let out a soft bark.

"Well, I would call that a success." Willow hopped up from the floor. "Would you like something to drink?"

"Do you, by any chance, have coffee?" I scratched behind Sammy's ears and stood to follow Willow into the kitchen.

"Um, this house never runs out of coffee."

"Ever?" I sat down on a barstool at the kitchen island.

"Ever." She grabbed the can of coffee from the cabinet. There was a yelp. I stood to get a better view of what had happened. Sammy was on the floor, and Holly and Cookie were on top of him. "Should we save him?"

"Nah, he's fine." I sat back down. "I wanted to apologize."

"For what." She set two mugs on the counter.

"Making things awkward earlier."

"It's okay. I get it." She filled the coffee maker and pressed the button to start the process.

"Get what?" Those two words confused me.

She sat down beside me. "We don't know each other. The kiss maybe shouldn't have happened."

"Yes, it should've." It was the first time I had felt something so wonderful in a long time.

"Oh, okay." She looked confused.

"I got into my head. Freaked myself out." I let out a heavy sigh. "It's been a while since I've felt those feelings you stirred up today."

"And that's a good thing?"

"Yeah." I turned to face her and grabbed her hand. "I guess I'm trying to say I'm a work in progress."

"Aren't we all?" She winked and hopped up to grab our coffee.

I felt a nudge against my leg. It was Sammy. "Hey, buddy. You okay?"

"Look." Willow set my mug down and pointed into the living room. Cookie and Holly were snuggled together on the floor, fast asleep.

"Wow." I grabbed my mug. Shouldn't the babies wear out the adult first? Sammy looks like he's ready for round two. A loud ringing startled the babies and made Sammy start barking. "Is that my phone?"

"It might be mine." Willow ran into the living room to retrieve her phone. "It's mine." She tapped her finger on the screen. "Molly, hey."

I couldn't hear the conversation. All I could see was Willow laughing.

She hung up the phone and walked back into the kitchen. "Do you own a Christmas-themed ugly sweater?"

"No, why?"

"You're going to need one." She set her phone on the granite countertop and sat down beside me.

"I'm afraid to ask."

"Molly and Anika are throwing an ugly Christmas sweater party." She sipped her coffee and wrapped her hands around the warm mug.

I rested my arm on the counter. "Do you have an ugly Christmas sweater?"

"Me, no." She laughed. "I don't even have Christmas decorations."

"You can have mine." I winked and took a sip of my coffee.

"Wait, you don't put up your Christmas decorations?" Her eyes went wide.

"Why does that shock you?"

"Everyone in this town gives off a Christmas vibe." She shrugged. "I have this vision that every house in Crystal Shores has a shit ton of decorations covering every inch of their property, inside and out."

"I mean, yeah, a lot do decorate, but many people don't." A conversation between Anika and Molly at the bar popped into my mind for some reason. They had been discussing throwing a party. I couldn't remember if the words ugly Christmas sweater were part of the discussion, though.

"This is my year of change. Maybe I need to get a little crazy and buy a tree." She looked over at the sleeping babies and burst out laughing. "Or not."

"What? You worried about the babies destroying it?"

"Um, yeah."

"Sammy used to love it when we put a tree up. He would curl up under the tree and sleep there for hours." Memories of my ex clouded my mind.

"I have an idea." She placed her hand on my forearm. "I'll put up a tree. Sammy can come over and sleep under my tree, and maybe..."

"He'll teach the babies about sleeping under it peacefully instead of destroying it." I leaned forward and almost kissed Willow. We were a breath apart, and I froze. It took me a few seconds before I finally sat back on the barstool.

There was something about her; she made me feel so comfortable and happy.

TWELVE

WILLOW

Two days later...

"Tell me again why you're throwing an ugly Christmas sweater party?" I was kneading the stollen bread. "Why can't it be a Christmas party, minus the ugly sweater?"

"Because." Anika grabbed an empty sheet pan off the rolling rack.

"Because why?" I knew I sounded like a two-year-old, but I was curious.

"Because they're so much fun." Molly stepped into the kitchen, holding a bowl of lemons. "If everyone plays fair, the sweaters are so ugly and hilarious."

"Do the clothing stores here carry some ugly sweaters?" We only had a few clothing stores in town. You had to drive up to Traverse City or order online to do extensive shopping.

"They do, but not enough." Molly grabbed a Microplane and zested the lemons. "If people show up to the party wearing the same sweater, we usually find out they shopped at the local stores."

"When's the party?" I set the bowl of dough in the proofer.

"Next weekend." Anika stepped up beside me and bumped her hip against mine. "You're not trying bail already, are you?"

"Well, it did cross my mind." I made sure to look at her when I rolled my eyes. "Actually, I'm thinking about ordering something online."

"What? Why?" Molly tapped the Microplane on the side of the bowl. "Shopping during the holidays is the best part of the season."

"For you." Whenever I thought about Christmas or decorating, I was taken back to a time when I was with my family. There was nothing happy about those memories. "But don't worry, I'll find a sweater before the big day."

Molly made a tsking sound and stepped closer to me. "Okay, I'm about to talk about things you hate to discuss."

"Um, okay." I knew she meant my family.

"I'm getting the vibe you're not into the holiday season." She moved loose flour around the prep table with her index finger. "Does that mean you don't decorate, too?"

Anika sat down beside us on the little stool. "Wait, is that true?"

I let out a heavy sigh and leaned my hip against the table. "The holiday season brings back a lot of bad memories for me."

Molly reached for my hand. "I'm not going to dredge up the shitty stuff. All I will say is you keep saying this is the year of change. If that's true, you should go out with a bang."

Anika grabbed my other hand. "She's not wrong. If you want to make serious changes, you should do something big for the holiday season."

"Big?" I turned my head to the side, curious about what big meant.

"Big." Molly lifted my hand and tugged me into the center of the room to spin me around. "So big, as in hanging lights and bulbs on a tree. Then, let your new fur babies attempt to destroy all the hard work. That big." I stepped closer to her and dropped my forehead onto her shoulder. "Oh, sweetie." She pulled me close and wrapped her arms around me.

"Willow," Anika said and wrapped her body around me.

"This one is going to be hard," I mumbled into Molly's shoulder. "Andy was at my house the other day; we talked about how I should get a tree so his dog and my two crazy kids can enjoy it together." They both stepped back. "What?"

"Andy was at your house?" Molly's eyes went wide, and she glanced over at Anika.

"Yeah, why?"

"Andy, um, hasn't been interested in a person of the opposite sex since his ex left. I love that he's spending time with you." Anika plopped back down on the stool. "Talk about big; *that's* big."

Our kiss popped into my mind.

"Why are you blushing?" Molly lightly pushed at my shoulder.

"We also may have kissed in the shed when trying to untangle the lights." I grabbed another stool and sat down beside Anika. "It was..."

"Magical." Molly grabbed a stool and sat right in front of us.

"Everything you dreamed of." Anika sighed.

"No, but it was perfect." I knew I was grinning ear to ear.

"Why am I sensing a but?" Molly laughed.

"He made things awkward afterward, which is why he was at my place with his dog, Sammy. He wanted to apologize, and the apology led to him meeting my new furry kids at my place." I shrugged.

Anika grabbed Molly's hand. "Um."

"Yeah–" Molly shook Anika's hand– "I know."

"What?" I rolled my eyes.

"The way Andy's ex left was awful." Molly let go of Anika's hand and ran up front. A minute later, Molly returned, holding a plate with lemon bars. "Here." She set the plate on the prep table and sat on the stool. "All his close friends didn't know if he would date again; that's how bad things have been."

"Oh." I grabbed a lemon bar. "I knew about the ex but didn't know all the details." I took a bite. "Huh." I rested my hand holding the lemon bar on my thigh. "Okay, you both need to help me with something."

"Anything." Molly squeezed my thigh.

"What she said." Anika winked.

"I want to enjoy the holiday season for the first time, like truly feel it." My chest tightened, and tears pricked the corner of my eyes. "Will you share everything you love about Christmas and help me to let go of the past with new traditions?" I said the word new, and a tear slid down my cheek.

Molly and Anika pulled me to the standing position and held me tight.

Molly leaned back a few inches. "We should start by getting you a tree." She giggled. "Those two furry babies will go crazy, but that's also the fun part of the holiday season."

When the topic of Christmas started, I wanted to run and hide.

Now, I felt excited to discover new traditions and let go of the ugly memories.

Plus, if I put a tree up, maybe Andy and his dog, Sammy, would come over again.

"First, we need to find you an ugly Christmas sweater." Molly placed her hand on Anika's shoulder. "Are you thinking what I'm thinking?"

"Road trip." Anika hopped up and down.

Putting my finger on Crystal Shores was the best happy accident.

I burst out laughing. "Fine. Let's do it."

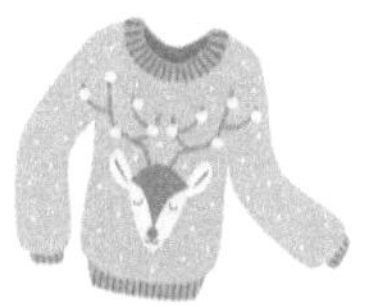

WILLOW

"Willow." I heard Andy's voice behind me.

I spun around. "Andy." I turned my head to the side. "Fancy meeting you here."

"Don't tell me you're shopping for an ugly Christmas sweater, too?" He laughed and took a few steps closer.

"I am." I giggled. "Who roped you into coming up here?"

"My mom." He shrugged. "My family lives here. When I mentioned the party, she started going on and on about all the ugly sweaters she had seen when shopping." He held up a bag he was holding. "Don't tell her, but I grabbed the first one I saw."

"You're not a fan of shopping either?" I held up my bag.

"This may sound rude, but I thought women loved to shop."

"Not all of them." I winked.

"Noted. Are you here by yourself?"

I pointed to the store behind me. "Anika and Molly are still looking at a few things.

"Oh, okay." He had this look like he wanted to ask me something. "I guess I'll see you back in Crystal Shores."

"Unless." I paused and glanced over my shoulder. Anika and Molly picked me up and had a full day of fun planned. A part of me wanted to enjoy the rest of the day with them, but the other part wanted to spend some time with Andy.

"Unless you two go off and do something together." Molly wrapped her arm around my bicep. "Hey, Andy."

"Hey." He smiled. "I was just heading home."

"Are you sure about that?" Anika winked.

He held up his keys. "Well, yeah, but I'm not in a hurry."

"Are you sure?" I whispered so only Molly could hear. "You had a full day planned."

Molly leaned in and kissed my cheek. "Go. It will be good for the both of you." She made sure to whisper, too. Then, a little louder, she said, "Our fun day isn't ending." She reached for Anika's hand. "We're going to go get a pasty."

There was this awkward pause between us.

"No pressure–" Andy looked over at me– "but if you want, we could get some dinner."

I turned to Molly. "I feel bad."

"Don't." She pushed me toward Andy. "Go have fun."

Anika stepped closer to Molly. "It's okay." She blew me a kiss.

"Well, you heard them." I shrugged my shoulders and took a few steps closer to Andy.

"I did." He smiled and reached out his hand. "Have you ever had dessert before dinner?"

"Um, no, but I'm very interested." I took his

outstretched hand. "Do you have something in mind?" I waved goodbye to Molly and Anika.

"Are you a chocolate fan?" He squeezed my hand.

"Not necessarily a fan, but I do like it." I thought he would release my hand. Instead, he tugged me closer to his body, and we walked hand in hand. After learning more about Andy, my time with him felt special. "I love a good chocolate cake."

"Then we're heading to the right place." He bumped his shoulder against mine. "It's crazy we ran into each other."

"Did Molly or Anika share we would be up here?" I found it weird that we managed to go shopping on the same day.

"No, but Julian did give me the day off, which is unusual." He stopped in the middle of the sidewalk. "Do you think it's possible..."

"...they devised a plan for us to run into each other? Um, yes." I laughed at the thought.

"Especially if Molly was involved." Andy shook his head.

"Is that okay?" I decided it was better to ask before my feelings for him multiplied.

"Is what, okay?" He stopped and turned to face me. "You and I running into each other?"

"Yeah, if I'm holding you up from anything, I don't want to get in the way." I suddenly felt myself plunged back in time and talking to my mom. I had always felt like I was a bother to her.

"Hey." He opened the door to a little cafe. "Let's get some chocolate cake and talk." I stared at the door briefly before sighing heavily and walked inside. "You couldn't say no to the cake, eh?"

"Maybe." I smiled. The place was tiny, but the display

case was packed with pastries. On one end of the display were three shelves and several different cakes. "Wow."

"Right." He placed the palm of his hand on the small of my back. "It doesn't matter what you get; everything is amazing here."

"Back already." A woman rested her hands on the top of the display case.

"Stella, stop sharing my secrets." He winked at me. "I didn't know we would run into each other."

"So, you're having two desserts before dinner." I laughed and walked the length of the case. "Can I get two things?"

"Honey, you can have as much as you like." The woman winked.

"I know he loves the chocolate cake. What is your favorite?" I couldn't take my eyes off the cherry and straw-berry fruit tarts.

"I like to keep things simple. The cherry strudel is my favorite item on the menu." She pointed at the strudels.

"Okay, let's do this." I turned toward Andy. "I had a friend growing up who loved to try all the desserts. She would get a little of each option; it was the perfect way to taste all of them. Of course, that may be difficult here, but let's get a box and add several sweets." I pointed at the cherry and strawberry tart. "I want what you both suggested, and that looks amazing."

Andy nodded. "You heard the woman. We need a box; let's get a dozen sweets."

"Can that include a piece of chocolate cake?" I made my way over to the cakes.

"For you, yes." Stella grabbed a different box and added a slice of cake.

Once I picked out a baker's dozen assortment of

pastries, we found a table in the corner, away from every-one. I held up the forks. "Should we get plates?"

"Or, we can eat them straight out of the box." Andy pulled out my chair—such a gentleman.

"Andy, this may be the beginning of a wonderful friend-ship." I opened the box and bent closer to inhale the aroma. "You know what I'm thinking about right now?"

"Which one you should try first?" He opened the second box with the piece of cake.

"Well, yes, but how have I never had dessert before dinner?" I plunged my fork down into the cake. "Wait, is that black forest cake?"

"Yup. Everything is better with cherries." I shoved the too-large piece into my mouth and covered it with my hand. All I could do was moan. "I know. Amazing, right?"

It was delicious, and I was beginning to see how wonderful the man who suggested the cake was, too.

FOURTEEN

ANDY

"How did Molly convince you to shop for an ugly sweater?" I had run to grab a plastic knife to cut off a piece of the cherry strawberry tart.

Willow was in the middle of chewing. She shook her head from side to side and finished the bite. "Hmmm... should I share the full story?"

"That depends."

"On what?"

"Are you comfortable sharing it?" I took a drink of my coffee. "No pressure."

"Well, to be honest, it's because of you." She set her fork down and leaned back against the chair.

"Me? How? Why?" I didn't mean to scowl. "I'm very curious now."

I couldn't get Willow out of my mind for the last few days. It was a good feeling. One I had missed. My ex had clouded my judgment for way too long. Willow helped me to see it was time to move forward.

"I guess you could say decorating the downtown area

with you made me think about the holidays differently." She moved a napkin back and forth with her index finger.

"Wait, does that mean you're putting up a Christmas tree?" I held my mug up for the waitress to refill my coffee. "Thank you."

"I think that's on the list." She smiled.

"Whoa, back up." I set my mug down and rested my forearms on the table. "There's a list?"

"Yup. Starts with the sweater. Then, the tree happens, and I guess there will be baking gingerbread cookies somewhere in there, too." She grabbed a forkful of the cake. "Now that I'll have a tree, you can bring Sammy over."

"Holly and Cookie are going to go crazy." I tried to hold in my laugh, but the vision was too good.

"Yeah, Molly's already preparing me." She shrugged. "It's just stuff. It'll be okay."

"You know what?"

"What?"

"We could go get your tree on the way home."

She cut a piece of the strudel. "Don't you have plans?"

"To get a tree. Yes." She leaned back in the chair and turned her head toward the big bay window. "What? It looks like you're thinking really hard over there."

She laughed and dropped her head. "I don't want to be a bother."

"To whom?"

"You, Molly, everyone."

I reached my hand forward and placed it on hers. "Hey, if it were a bother, we wouldn't suggest it." She lifted her head, and I could see tears forming in the corners of her eyes. "Did someone make you feel that way from your past?"

"Yeah." She wiped away the tears before they had a chance to fall. "Sometimes it's hard to let go."

"Yeah, it is." I had no room to judge; I had been living in the past with my ex since she walked out the door. "Crystal Shores is different."

"How so?" She took a sip of her coffee.

"The people who are from here, don't judge." I shrugged. "They look forward to giving back."

She placed her elbow on the table and rested her chin on her closed hand. "I have noticed that." She looked right at me. "I'm glad we ran into each other today."

"Me, too." I held my mug up, and she grabbed hers to tap against mine.

"If I get a tree, you have to get one, too." She winked.

I wanted to say no, but I was excited by the thought. After decorating the downtown area with her, putting up a tree with Willow would be pretty magical.

"I think that can be arranged."

"Really?" Her eyes went wide.

"Yeah, really."

She reached for her fork. "One more bite to celebrate, and then I need to close the box."

"I don't know if I can eat another bite." This was my second time having dessert in less than two hours.

"Just one." She grabbed a forkful of browned butter cherry blondie.

"One." I sighed and sunk my fork into the blondie.

Two hours later...

"Sammy is going to be so happy." Willow turned in her

seat to face me. "Do you have bulbs and lights for your tree?"

We stopped on the way home and got two trees currently tied to my vehicle's roof.

"No." My ex had taken all the Christmas decorations. Before leaving, she commented that I never helped with decorations, so she might as well take them.

"Then we have one more stop to make." She clapped her hands together and flashed the biggest smile.

"You're really excited?"

"I know, it's weird, but I am." She rubbed her hands up and down her thighs. "I took a picture of the trees on the roof for Molly and Anika. They keep sending GIFs to show their excitement." She laughed. "The silly videos are changing my mood."

"I know at first I sounded like the Grinch, but the truth is, decorating *is* fun." I turned into the parking lot of a shopping mall. "Do you want white or multi-color lights on the tree?"

"Multi-color, of course." She zipped her jacket up. "What about you?"

"Same." I put the car in park. "I love all the different bulbs and colorful lights."

"That sounds perfect." She placed her hand on the door handle. "Andy. Thank you."

"For what?" I hopped out and walked around to her side to open her door.

"Everything." She grabbed my outstretched hand. "I didn't realize how fun the holiday season could be."

I opened the door to the little store. "Just wait until you make cookies." She glanced back, and I was taken aback by how her face lit up at the mention of cookies.

Molly and Anika had done something special for Willow; they brought back the Christmas spirit.

It was time to learn how to bake because there was no way I was missing out on making gingerbread cookies with Willow.

"Gingerbread house competition." I blurted out the thought.

"Um, are you adding something to the list?" She wrapped her arm around my bicep and rested her head on my shoulder.

"Maybe." I pulled her closer, loving the way she felt next to me.

FIFTEEN

WILLOW

"Holy shit." I bolted from my bed and ran down the hall. "Cookie. Holly. Are you okay?"

My mom used to get upset at me because she said I could sleep through anything. What she meant was that I never heard her when she repeatedly yelled my name to wake up. If I didn't respond immediately, she made it seem like I was an inconvenience and disrupting her time.

The truth: I was a hard sleeper. I had vivid dreams and didn't get up much through the night to go to the bathroom. When my head hit the pillow, I was out.

That had changed, though.

Cookie and Holly were very busy at all hours of the day. I talked with them about when it's dark out, it's time to sleep. I think they heard that when it's dark, they should have fun running around and making a lot of noise.

"Oh." I stood in the middle of the living room and burst out laughing. "Well, Molly, Anika, and Andy called this one."

The Christmas tree Andy and I had spent so much time

decorating was now on its side on the floor. There were broken bulbs and strands of lights that had fallen off the tree and were lying in a pile under the tree.

Cookie was lying flat on the floor with her head on her front paws. Her eyes looked so sad.

Holly had lights tangled around her body and was stuck in the very center of the tree.

I plopped down on the floor in front of Cookie. "Well, do you feel better now?" Cookie whimpered and inched closer to me. "Do you think we should rescue Holly?" At the mention of her name, Holly meowed at a volume I had never heard before. "Okay, okay, hold on. I got you." I carefully unwound the lights from her body and pulled her onto my lap. "You two. I tell ya." Cookie climbed up onto my lap next to Holly. "Do you want to help me put the tree back up?" Cookie's tail started to wag, and Holly rubbed her head against my leg. "Okay, let's do it."

It took a few hours to get the tree back up and redecorated. Once the tree was stable, they curled into a ball under the branches and fell asleep. I continued to decorate while they slept. At least someone would get a good night's sleep.

At around 1:30 am, I finally went back to bed. Hopefully, the tree would still be up in the morning.

They were lucky they were cute.

Plus, it was just stuff. The tree and everything on it was replaceable.

I didn't have to get up early, so I let myself sleep in for a couple of extra hours.

Lately, my alarm clock was two fur babies on my chest, anxious for me to wake up. Today, I woke up alone.

"Okay–" I was ready to find the tree on the floor again when I stepped into the living room– "wow, it's still standing." Cookie and Holly lifted their heads and stretched before greeting me. "So, now you like the tree, huh?"

Cookie hopped up and down while circling my legs. Holly sat down in front of me and meowed nonstop.

I sat down and crossed my legs in front of me. "Hey, come here." I patted my legs, and they both hopped up. "Do you know what day it is?" Cookie licked my hand, and Holly stared at me. "Yup, exactly, it's Saturday, which means the ugly Christmas sweater party is tonight." I scratched behind their ears. "I've made it through most of the list, but just two more items need to be crossed off. Can you guess what they are?" Cookie nudged her nose against my hand. "If that means wearing the ugly sweater and making a gingerbread house, then yes." I bent and kissed them both on the top of their head. My phone pinged with a new text message. "Okay, I need to grab that. Time to get up." I set them both on the floor, hopped up, and ran to grab my phone.

Andy: So, status?

For the last two days, Andy had sent me a text message to check on the status of the tree. Was it down or up?

Me: Well, right now it's up.
Andy: Right now. What does that mean?
Me: Last night, I woke up to a crash.
Andy: *Laughing Emoji*

Me: Laugh it up. It was crazy, and I'm exhausted, so I won't be able to go to the party tonight.
Andy: Wait, calling you.

A second later, my phone rang.

"Really? You're not going?" He sounded surprised. "Why would a tree falling over prevent you from attending a Christmas party?"

It was hard to hold in my laugh. He sounded so confused.

"I think you cheated by calling me." I giggled.

"What? Cheated? I'm lost." He let out a heavy sigh.

"I was messing with you." I sat on the floor and let the babies hop back on my lap. "Actually, Cookie, Holly, and I were just talking about how I have two items left on the list."

"Man, that's good because I didn't want to be the one to tell Molly you weren't coming." He let out a breath.

"Good point." I envisioned Molly getting in her car and driving to my house. She wouldn't care about excuses. "Don't worry." I smiled and booped Cookie's nose. "It was a mess last night, and several bulbs were lost, but I'll be there ready to celebrate when the list is complete."

"Just two items, eh? Tell me something."

"What's that?"

"Did the list do its job?"

By job, I knew he meant. Did it bring back the Christmas spirit I had lost so long ago? "Does this answer your question—When I woke up this morning, I was excited to make eggnog pancakes and peppermint hot chocolate."

"You may have tipped the scale by adding peppermint to your hot chocolate."

"Should I dial it back a bit?"

"Nah, have fun." He laughed. "Plus, peppermint hot chocolate is delicious."

We chatted for a few more minutes. Before we hung up, he offered to bring some extra bulbs for my tree to replace the broken ones. Damn, I loved this small town.

SIXTEEN

ANDY

"I thought you and Willow would be arriving together." Molly leaned against the doorframe and had this confused look on her face.

"Well, hello to you, too." I took a step forward and kissed her cheek. "We only talked about meeting here. I could've picked her up." She swatted her hand against my arm. "Ow, what was that for?"

"She mentioned something about you being a perfect gentleman." She rolled her eyes and turned to head into the kitchen.

"What does that mean?" I followed behind her.

"A perfect gentleman picks the lady up so she doesn't have to drive."

"No, no, wait a minute." Jackson, Anika's boyfriend, interjected. "Are you officially dating?"

"I mean, not officially, but maybe, I don't know." We had been talking more, but I didn't know if it was fair to say we were in the dating category.

"They're dating." Anika covered Jackson's mouth.

"Um, define dating?" Jackson grabbed Anika's hand and tugged her closer to his body.

"Willow told us you talk every day." She glanced my way for confirmation.

"That's true. I've been checking in to see if the tree was destroyed." I shrugged. "She didn't know how the new kitten and puppy would react."

Jackson scowled. "And?"

"And what?" I didn't know what else to say.

"Have you been on an actual date?" Jackson grabbed a chip and dipped it into some dip.

"Yeah, I took her to Razem." I leaned my hand on the counter. "Once for August's special hot chocolate and then for dinner."

"And you both looked very cozy together." August stepped into the room and shoved his hands in his pants pockets.

The room erupted in laughter.

"You're dating." Jackson held his hand up. "Like it or not, it's happening."

"You like it, right?" Molly wrapped her arm around my bicep.

"Um, yeah." I glanced down at her. "I'm enjoying my time with her." The doorbell rang. Hopefully, it was Willow. I needed a distraction. "It might be Willow; I'll grab it."

In unison, everyone said, "Ohhhhhh." I held my middle finger up as I left the room.

There was a little window on the right side of the door. It was Willow. I swung the door open and burst out laughing. "How?"

She glanced at her sweater and then at me. "Wait, how is that possible?"

"I bought my sweater a few hours before we ran into each other."

"This is insane." She stepped inside.

Molly ran down the hall to greet Willow. "Hey–" she looked over at me and back at Willow– "Um..."

"I didn't consult with him. You were there when I bought my sweater." She held her hands up. "This is crazy."

"What's wrong?" Anika stepped into the small space and burst out laughing. "We took a trip to Traverse City to avoid this. How the hell did you buy the same ugly sweater?"

"Does that mean they are disqualified from the competition?" Jackson was standing at the end of the hallway next to the kitchen.

"Oh, hush." Molly and Anika grabbed a stuffed Santa and Mrs. Claus to throw at him.

I stepped closer to Willow. "Well, this is a fun twist on the day."

"Ya think." She laughed and grabbed my hand to head into the kitchen.

The kitchen was big but felt small, with a room full of people.

Anika, Jackson, Molly, Jasper, Mack, August, Julian, Eddie, Sarah, Holland, Jen, Chef Nolan, Jake, Milo, and Angie were all invited. It took everyone a few minutes to greet Willow.

"Okay, now that everyone is here." Molly rubbed her hands together. "It's time to make gingerbread houses. We have enough supplies to make four houses, so break up into teams of four or five people."

Willow and I were on Mack, August, and Julian's team, which was awkward. I still had no idea if August and Mack were dating. Did Julian know about the kiss?

"She's timing us?" Willow had her hand on a cookie for the side of the house.

"Molly is serious about competitions." My hand was on the container of frosting. "That's why she won the Crystal Shores pie contest six years in a row. Have you seen the Welcome to Crystal Shores sign when you drive into town?"

"Home of the chocolate lemon chess pie. It's my favorite pie at the bakery."

"Yup, it's also her most famous recipe."

Once Molly blew the whistle, everyone was frantically trying to assemble the gingerbread houses. Cookies fell on the floor, candy scattered in all directions, and frosting ended up on our faces, hands, and sweaters.

August had accidentally dropped the cookies for the roof, so we were immediately disqualified. I pulled out a chair for Willow to sit and watch the rest of the teams work against the clock to make the most unique house.

"Time," Molly yelled sixty minutes later.

"Hey," I bent down and whispered in Willow's ear. "Can we talk?"

She glanced up at me and smiled. "Of course." We walked hand in hand into the living room. "Everything okay?"

It was still loud in the living room from laughter. It would take a village to clean up the mess we had just created.

"More than okay." I took a step closer and grabbed her other hand. "I wanted to say thank you."

"For what?" She smiled.

"Well, I know you had a list to complete."

"And it is officially all checked off." She jumped up and down with excitement.

"I didn't have a list, but if I did, it would have one item on the list."

"Oh, yeah." She squeezed my hands. "What would that item be?"

"To let go of the past."

She dropped her head and nodded. "Yeah, I feel that." She lifted her head. "So."

"What?"

"Did you let it go?"

"It took some extra work, but I believe I did." I winked. "Eating too many pastries in Traverse City sealed the deal."

She groaned. "I'm still full. Why didn't you stop me from overeating?"

"Would you have stopped if I said something?"

"No." She burst out laughing. "That browned butter cherry blondie still brings a tear to my eye."

"We'll have to go on a road trip and get more." I moved a strand of hair behind her ear.

"That would be wonderful." She rested her hands on my chest. "I should probably say thank you, too."

"Oh, what for?"

"Never in my wildest dreams did I think I could fall in love with Christmas." She slid her hand up and looped it around my neck. "I thought it was impossible to find the Christmas spirit again. I'm glad you all proved me wrong."

"Me, too." I bent and captured her lips.

"Wait." She leaned back a few inches and placed her index finger over my lips. "I need to share one more secret with you."

"Okay." I turned my head to the side, curious about what it could be.

"Well, I think it's pretty obvious: your sweater is uglier than mine."

"We're wearing the same sweater."

"I see a few differences. Plus–" she stepped out of my embrace– "you must admit, it looks way better on me."

I tried to reach forward and tickle her side, but she ran to the other side of the room. We chased each other for a few minutes until she stumbled and fell onto the couch. I was right on her heels, so I slipped and fell on top of her. "I give up; you look better in the sweater." I brushed my nose back and forth over hers.

She placed her hands on either side of my face. "There is something we can agree on."

"Tell me." I kissed her.

"We look better happy." She kissed me.

"Yeah, you do." Molly and Anika cheered.

WANT TO MEET THE CRYSTAL SHORES CHARACTERS?

Light My Heart (Crystal Shores Book 1)

Guard My Heart (Crystal Shores Book 2)

Defend My Heart (Crystal Shores Book 3)

Cherish My Heart (Crystal Shores Book Serial)

A NOTE FROM THE AUTHOR

How is it possible that they bought the same ugly sweater?

Do you agree that their friends and family were all playing Match Maker?

I have a love for Hallmark movies. Writing Willow and Andy's story with all those loving movies in mind was so much fun.

This book was a standalone novella, but that doesn't mean it will be the last time you see them.

I'll let you head on over to Crystal Shores to meet the other characters in the book.

Sending love and donuts, Terra

You can read the first book in the Crystal Shores Series with the QR code below.

Light My Heart (Crystal Shores Book 1)

Join my newsletter–We talk about books, recipes, gardening, crocheting, lettering, drawing, animals, and so much more.

You'll get a front-row seat on new chapters released for each book serial, book updates, blog posts, and new recipes.

Once you join, you'll find a few treats waiting for you as a thank-you for joining!

You can sign up at terrakelly.com or use the QR code below.

Join my newsletter here!

ABOUT TERRA KELLY

Hi there! This is me, Terra Kelly, a romance author, food blogger, and creative who loves lettering, drawing, crocheting, and gardening.

This is my husband, cat–Juno, and two bunnies–Lavender & Earl Grey.

Welcome to our home and favorite place to relax and create together in Charlotte, North Carolina.

I love writing sweet romance, steamy romance, and romantic suspense.

All my books are available in eBook and paperback format on my website or in your favorite online bookstore and libraries.

That's not all, though.

You can also read a new chapter weekly in the Crystal

Shores serial and a new chapter every other week in the No Rules Required serial. Join our community on Ream and start reading today.

As an extra treat, I add recipes to my books or share recipes on my blog inspired by the characters in my books.

The characters think of the recipes, and I run to the kitchen to create the delicious treat.

I started a food blog in 2010 and published my first book in 2014. Combining these two passions in one space just made sense.

The food blog has changed over the years because my food needs have changed.

In 2025, most of my recipes will use whole wheat flour. You'll also see less sugar and more sugar alternatives.

Reading romance isn't just about reading words on a page; it's also about building around the story and the characters. That includes the recipes they made, what's in their garden, and so much more.

I can't wait for you to meet my characters and enjoy the delicious recipes they love to make for YOU!

Join the fun!
www.terrakelly.com
chatwithterra@terrakelly.com

Want Steamy Romance?

MAN CARD SERIES

CRYSTAL SHORES SERIES

THE WINTERS FAMILY SERIES

HANNAH'S STORY: A SECOND CHANCE

SWEET TREATS TO GO BUNDLE

Want Romantic Suspense?

FIGHT IT OUT SERIES

THE FALLING TRILOGY

**Check out other books by Terra Kelly
on her website at terrakelly.com**

ACKNOWLEDGMENTS

In October 2024, I decided to write a Christmas story that would be released two months later. After a rough couple of years, I wanted to share something with YOU before the year ended, even if it was a last-minute decision. It was time to share a new book and get us excited for more.

Thank you to my angel, my beautiful husband. I love how we work together. He jumps in and offers the perfect ideas when I struggle with a detail.

Sending a big hug and kiss to my furry babies. My cat Juno loves to sit against my chest with part of her body next to the keyboard. You could say she keeps the inspiration flowing with her all her purring. My bunnies, Lavender and Earl Grey, are the perfect distraction when I need to think about what to write next.

Thank you, The Word Fairy, for your awesome editing and for spending time with me to make the book gorgeous.

Thank you to my fans and readers. Your support makes this adventure so much better.

Thank you to my friends and family for all your support and love.

Copyright 2024 Terra Kelly

Your Sweater is Uglier Than Mine
Small-Town Romantic Comedy

Ebook Edition
Amazon, Apple Books, Barnes and Noble, Kobo, Libraries, and More...

Cover Art by Terra Kelly

 Formatted with Vellum